Dirt
on My
Shirt

JEFF FOXWORTHY

Dirt on My Shirt

Illustrated by STEVE BJÖRKMAN

HarperCollins Publishers

Look carefully at the picture for the poem What Do You See? and see if you can find the following: acorns, ants, bear, bees, birds, bunny, butterflies, caterpillar, centipedes, chipmunk, clouds, crayfish, deer, dragonfly, fish, flies, fox, frog, gopher, grasshopper, ladybug, lizard, mice, moon, raccoon, skunk, snail, snake, spider, squirrels, tadpoles, turtle, worm.

Dirt on My Shirt

Copyright © 2008 by Jeff Foxworthy

Printed in the U.S.A.

For information address HarperCollins Children's Books, a division of HarperCollins Publishers, 1350 Avenue of the Americas, New York, NY 10019.

www.harpercollinschildrens.com

Library of Congress Cataloging-in-Publication Data is available.
ISBN 978-0-06-120846-1 (trade bdg.) — ISBN 978-0-06- 120847-8 (lib. bdg.)

Typography by Rachel Zegar

8 9 10

❖

First Edition

For Maggie, ever the encourager and always a friend.

Thank you for nudging me down this path.

—J.F.

To the students at Greentree Elementary

and their dedicated principal, Dianne Ball.

—S.B.

Dirt on My Shirt

There's dirt on my shirt
And leaves in my hair
There's mud on my boots
But I don't really care

Playing outside is so much fun
To breathe the clean air
And feel the warm sun

To stomp in a puddle
Or climb a big tree
Makes me quite happy
Just look and you'll see

Lost Hat

I lost my favorite hat, I don't know where it's at

I looked around my room, I looked beneath the cat

I looked beside the bathtub, I looked under the sink

Where did I leave my hat? I tried and tried to think

I thought I might have left it by the TV in the den

It wasn't there, so I went back and checked my room again

About to cry, I found my mom. "I've lost my hat," I said

She smiled and said, "I found it. It's sitting on your head!"

Are We There Yet?

The Jenkins went out for a ride
"How much longer?" the children cried
"A while!" their dad said with regret
"We haven't left the driveway yet!"

Staring Contest

I am staring at my cat
He doesn't bat an eye
Watching me, watching him
The seconds tick on by
Tears come to my eyes
I'm going to have to blink
He smiles a silly cat smile
And then gives me a wink

Missing

I had a tadpole in a bowl
But now he's disappeared
Where he swam a frog now sits
I think that's kinda weird

Hide-and-Seek

We caught a turtle down by the creek
Her shell is bumpy and gray
We don't mean to scare her
But when we get near her
Her head and her legs go away!

Bumblebee Breakfast

Bumblebees like doughnut trees
The sugar's sweet and sticky
But do not eat the ones that fall
'Cause dirt and ants taste icky!

Deer

An eye

Then an ear

I think I see a deer

Hiding behind that big tree

A stomp

Then a flash

And he's gone in a dash

I think the deer just saw me

Spare Hair

Salamander sitting there
Salamander has no hair
His friend the bear has hair to spare
But bear won't share
And that's not fair!

True Love

Cows have horns that don't go beep
Dads have sweaters, so do sheep
Turtles have tails that they can't see
I have you and you have me

Uninvited Guests

Atop our bird feeder's a squirrel we call Peter
Who's eating seeds meant for others
The birds are concerned, because they just learned
He's invited his sisters and brothers!

Friends

Friends come in all colors
And sizes and shapes
Friends share their jump ropes
And friends share their grapes
They like the same jokes
And they like the same shows
They lend you their ear
And they lend you their clothes
A world without friends
I don't think I could bear it
Life is much better
With good friends to share it

Choices

Pick a color

Pick a number

Pick a place to hide

Pick a flower

Pick a pear

Pick a horse to ride

Wishing and Fishing

I was just wishing that I could go fishing

What I might catch I don't know

A shark or a whale, or a fish with no tail

No matter 'cause I'll let 'em go

Noises

"Boing, boing, boing" goes a happy kangaroo

"Boing, boing, boing" goes a hoppy frog too

"Yip, yip, yip" goes the puppy up the street

"Tweet, tweet, tweet" goes our little parakeet

"Ding-a-ling-a-ling" goes a fire truck in a hurry

"Wah, wah, wah" goes my baby brother Murray

Bubbles

I like to play and splash and sing

When I take my bath

But it's the bubbles that I make myself

That always make me laugh!

Roly-poly

I found a Roly-poly

He rolled into a ball

I rolled him through the kitchen

I rolled him down the hall

I rolled him to the back porch

He did not want to play

I went inside for dinner

And my Poly walked away

What Do You See?

What do you see when you look in the lake?

A turtle, a tadpole, a fish, or a snake?

What do you see when you look at the sky?

A bird or the moon or a cloud passing by?

What do you see when you look at the ground?

An acorn, an ant, or a worm squirming round?

What do you see when you look up a tree?

Branches and leaves, a hive full of bees?

Making Friends

I have a best friend, his name's Tommy Huff
I think that we're friends 'cause we like to make stuff

We made a sandwich, we made a tree house
We made up a game called "squeak like a mouse"

We made a tent out of chairs and a sheet
We made up a dance called "crazy duck feet"

We made green Jell-O, then made ourselves giggle
By shaking our bowls and watching it wiggle

We made a go-cart that we didn't finish
And we made a face when we had to eat spinach

We made a mess or so said my mother
We had a fight but made up with each other

We made ourselves scared by telling ghost stories
And we had to sleep with his big sister Laurie

A friend makes you happy, a friend makes you better
A friend is a treasure to hold on to forever!

Snakes Alive!

I looked out the window and saw a snake

Crawling around in the yard

My dad tried to find it, but it got away

I don't think he looked very hard

Uncle Ed and Aunt Foo Foo

My Uncle Ed and Aunt Foo Foo
Are quite the crazy pair
He has big red cowboy boots
And she has big red hair

They love to go out dancing
They really are a sight
He twirls her 'cross the floor
A blur of red and white

Their house is small and cozy
It smells like chocolate cake
Its shelves are filled with little dolls
Aunt Foo Foo likes to make

Their dog is short and round
His name is Mister Benny
They have a cat named Ralph
He's black and white and skinny

When it's time to say good night
They all climb into bed
Benny sleeps inside Ed's boot
And Ralph on Foo Foo's head

Cousins

My cousin Boris sings in the chorus
He sings way off-key and he's loud
With a plug in each ear, his mom and dad cheer
For their son of whom they're so proud

My cousin Lizzy makes me so dizzy
She never stops spinning around
She once spun so long her balance was gone
And she couldn't get up off the ground

My cousin Lenny is real tall and skinny
It's hard, but he never complains
If he grows much more, he won't fit through the door
And his hair won't get wet when it rains

My cousin Jesse is really quite messy
With stuff dripping off of his chin
The food on his face looks so out of place
There's more on the outside than in!

Uncle Moe

My Uncle Moe has a big mustache

It's bushy as can be

When he stands up straight and tall

He looks just like a tree!

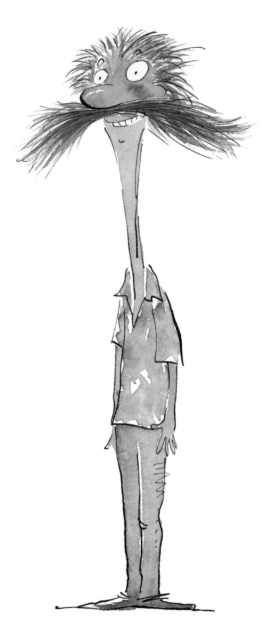

Uncle Keith

My Uncle Keith has great big teeth

He can eat corn really fast

My Grandma Rose has a really big nose

When she sneezes it's more like a blast

Uncle Larry

My Uncle Larry is really quite hairy

We giggle each time that he passes

We try not to stare, but he looks like a bear

Wearing shorts and goofy sunglasses

Auntie Brooke

My Auntie Brooke just loves to cook

From turkey to cookies to bread

When she makes spaghetti, you'd better get ready

For meatballs the size of your head!

She once made a cake as big as a lake

A cement truck stirred up the batter

She put on the icing that was so enticing

With the oar from a boat and a ladder

Grandma

My grandma puts on lipstick

It's bright red like a rose

Because she cannot see too well

It ends up on her nose!

Granddaddy

It sounds kind of sappy, but it makes me happy

To sit in my granddaddy's lap

He tickles, I giggles and wiggles like crazy

And sometimes we just like to nap

Summer Days

A grasshopper hops, a windmill stops

A bee buzzes along kissing flowers

These summer days are perfect in ways

Except for the afternoon showers

Escape

How happy are balloons that finally get away?

Escaped from little hands

That tried to make them stay

Where do they go, I wonder?

With no map to guide them

To Heaven I would guess

Where little angels ride them

Pretend

I sometimes pretend that my bed is a sled

My floor isn't carpet, it's ice cream instead

I sometimes pretend that my bed is a fort

My job is to watch and send a report

I sometimes pretend that my bed is a whale

I ride on his back, 'cross the oceans we sail

I sometimes pretend my bed is a cave

I huddle inside from the snow I am saved

I sometimes pretend that my bed is a rocket

I soar past the moon toward the planet Woosocket

I sometimes pretend that my pillow is you

I hug it so tight till the nighttime is through

Bobo Bye-Bye

On a tire swing Bobo sat

Swinging very high

He thought he'd let go of the rope

Tell Bobo bye-bye!

Sharing a Bed

Sharing a bed with your cousins

Is not the easiest thing

They toss and they turn

They giggle and snore

And sometimes

They just like to sing

In the Night

Ticktock goes the clock

Hanging on the wall

Dink dink goes the sink

Dripping 'cross the hall

Clop clop go the shoes

I hear my daddy walking

Ring ring goes the phone

I hear my mama talking

I need a drink of water

So down the hall I creep

I hear my mother calling

"Why aren't you asleep?!"